The Nastiest Drink in the World

Book and Lyrics by
Mark Loewenstern

Music by
John Gregor

Baker's Plays
c/o Samuel French, Inc.
45 West 25th Street
New York, NY 10010
bakersplays.com

RENTAL MATERIALS

An orchestration consisting of a **Piano/Vocal Score** will be loaned two months prior to the production ONLY on the receipt of the Licensing Fee quoted for all performances, the rental fee and a refundable deposit.

Please contact Samuel French for perusal of the music materials as well as a performance license application.

IMPORTANT BILLING AND CREDIT REQUIREMENTS

All producers of THE NASTIEST DRINK IN THE WORLD *must* give credit to the Author of the Play in all programs distributed in connection with performances of the Play, and in all instances in which the title of the Play appears for the purposes of advertising, publicizing or otherwise exploiting the Play and/or a production. The name of the Author *must* appear on a separate line on which no other name appears, immediately following the title and *must* appear in size of type not less than fifty percent of the size of the title type.

In addition the following credit *must* be given in all programs and publicity information distributed in association with this piece:

First produced at Vital Theatre Company
New York, New York

THE NASTIEST DRINK IN THE WORLD was first produced by the Vital Theatre Company. The performance was directed by Carrie Libling. The cast was as follows:

SAMANTHA . . . . Kelly Hayes

KING FREDIPUS . . . . Aaron Walters

PRIMO . . . . Matt Wells

SEGUNDA . . . . Dianna DiPalma

TERTIO . . . . Lee Overtree

UNDERSTUDY . . . . Craig Fitzpatrick

CHARACTERS

SAMANTHA - a shy young woman.

KING FREDIPUS - a young and spoiled king.

PRIMO - the king's anxious first advisor.

SEGUNDA - the king's overprotective second advisor.

TERTIO - the king's simple-minded third advisor.

SETTING

The Kingdom of Baloneya.

TIME

The Baloneyan Renaissance.

MUSICAL NUMBERS

The King is Always Right . . . .
PRIMO, SEGUNDA, TERTIO, KING FREDIPUS

Speak up, Samantha . . . .
SAMANTHA

The Nastiest Drink in the World . . . .
SAMANTHA, KING FREDIPUS

It's Great! . . . .
PRIMO, SEGUNDA, TERTIO, KING FREDIPUS

Sneeze Attack . . . .
SAMANTHA, KING FREDIPUS

Finale . . . .
ALL

(OVERTURE)

(At rise: Throne room. Upstage is a curtained window through which can be seen a small town with a clock tower.)

(Onstage is the Fantastical Juicing Cart (or FJC), an impressive piece of furniture holding many bottles, each filled with a colorful potion or powder. The centerpiece of the cart is a bowl for mixing ingredients.)

*(***PRIMO** *is onstage, ladling water from a bucket into the bottles of the FJC, until:)*

PRIMO. Oh, jellybeans! Out of water again.

(He crosses the stage with the bucket, but stops when he sees the audience. He's so startled that he drops the bucket.)

PRIMO. AHH! Dear me. Visitors. *(calling backstage)* Segunda, Tertio. Come quick! We have visitors.

*(***SEGUNDA** *and* **TERTIO** *enter.)*

SEGUNDA. Why, hello everyone.

TERTIO. Yeah, hello.

SEGUNDA. How delightful for you to pay us a visit. Is this the first time you've been to a palace? The King lives here, you know. Would you like to meet him?

PRIMO. Wait, wait, wait! Segunda, there's no time to entertain right now. First we have to finish rounding up the stink beetles His Highness created last week. And then I have to go all the way to the lake for water, because you know the King hasn't let it rain in three months and all the wells are dry. Even the Fantastical Juicing Cart is running low, and you know how grouchy the King gets when he hasn't had his mango juice. There's just so much work to do!

TERTIO. Yeah, Segunda. There's so much to do!

SEGUNDA. But first we must welcome our guests. Where's your manners, Primo?

TERTIO. Yeah, Primo. Manners.

(SONG 1: *"THE KING IS ALWAYS RIGHT"*)

SEGUNDA.

WELCOME TO BALONEYA,
THIRD KINGDOM EAST FROM ROME.
A LARKY LITTLE MONARCHY,
WE'RE PROUD TO CALL IT HOME.

TERTIO.

UH, WE'RE THE KING'S ADVISORS.
WE HELP WITH EVERY PLAN.
WE'RE ROYAL AND WE'RE LOYAL,
AND WE DO THE BEST WE CAN.

PRIMO.

THIS IS THE REGAL THRONE ROOM,
AND SOON, YOU'LL MEET THE KING.
BUT LISTEN CHUMS, BEFORE HE COMES,
YOU ALL MUST LEARN ONE THING:

SEGUNDA AND TERTIO. (*remembering*)

OH, YES! OH, YES!

ALL THREE.

EACH PERSON IN BALONEYA,
EACH LADY, LORD AND KNIGHT,
EACH KNAVE AND FOOL OBEYS THIS RULE:
THE KING IS ALWAYS RIGHT.

(*They reveal a sign which reads: "The King is Always Right."*)

ALL THREE.

IT'S THERE IN BLACK AND WHITE,
"THE KING IS ALWAYS RIGHT."

PRIMO.

AND HERE HE IS RIGHT NOW,
THE GRACIOUS, SMART, AND WONDERFUL,

SEGUNDA.

SAGACIOUS AND INFALLIBLE,

TERTIO.

THE MAN WHO IS THE HEAD OF US:

ALL THREE.

KING FREDIPUS!

(**KING FREDIPUS** *strides in magnificently.*)

KING FREDIPUS. *(spoken)* You must all be so honored to meet me!

(*He accidentally steps into* **PRIMO**'s *bucket. His legs spread wide and there is a loud ripping sound.*)

KING FREDIPUS.

I MEANT TO DO THAT.

(*He then turns upstage to mount his throne. His pants are torn, and his colorful boxer shorts are visible underneath.*)

TERTIO.

KING FREDIPUS?

KING FREDIPUS.

YES, TERTIO?

TERTIO.

IS THERE A PROBLEM WITH YOUR PANTS?

KING FREDIPUS.

WHAT DO YOU MEAN?

TERTIO.

A HOLE.

KING FREDIPUS.

A HOLE? IN MY PANTS?
IMPOSSIBLE. UNTHINKABLE.

TERTIO.

THAT'S WHAT I THOUGHT.

KING FREDIPUS.

AND WHAT'S MORE, NOT A CHANCE.
I KNOW WHICH CLOTHES I CHOSE TODAY
AND ON THEM IS NO HOLE OR FRAY.
THERE'S NO HOLE IN MY PANTS!

TERTIO. *(to audience)*

THE KING SAYS THERE'S NO HOLE.

KING FREDIPUS.

> NO SPLIT OR SLIT OR TEAR.

TERTIO.

> IT'S ME THAT'S WRONG IF ALL ALONG
> I SEE HIS UNDERWEAR.
>
> THE KING'S SO WISE, AND I'M SO DULL
> I WON'T BELIEVE MY SIGHT.
> COMPLY AND DON'T ASK WHY
> BECAUSE THE KING IS ALWAYS RIGHT.
>
> I'M REALLY NOT THAT BRIGHT,
> BUT THE KING IS ALWAYS RIGHT.

KING FREDIPUS.

> NO ONE'S EVER DISAGREED
> WITH ANY KING OR QUEEN.
> FROM LONG AGO RIGHT UP TO NOW,
> THAT'S HOW IT'S ALWAYS BEEN.
>
> (**SEGUNDA** *prepares to hang the national flag of Baloneya.*)

KING FREDIPUS.

> OH, SEGUNDA?

SEGUNDA.

> YES, MY DEAR SWEET HIGHNESS?

KING FREDIPUS.

> TAKE THAT BACK, SEGUNDA.
> I'VE DECIDED I NO LONGER WANT THAT FLAG.
> IT'S JUST TOO UNINSPIRING,
> SO TEDIOUS AND TIRING.
> EVERYTHING ABOUT IT IS A DRAG.
>
> (**KING FREDIPUS** *shows her another flag. It is of the king's face with a goofy expression.*)

KING FREDIPUS. *(spoken)* Surprise!

SEGUNDA. *(spoken)* I can't believe my eyes.

KING FREDIPUS.

> WHAT DO YOU THINK, SEGUNDA?
> ISN'T IT SENSATIONAL?

SEGUNDA.

WELL…

KING FREDIPUS.

YOU FIND IT INSPIRATIONAL?

SEGUNDA.

WELL…

KING FREDIPUS.

SHOULD IT GO HERE, OR ON THE TOWER?

SEGUNDA.

WELL…

KING FREDIPUS. *(hurt)*

WELL, I WORKED ON IT FOR ONE WHOLE HOUR!

SEGUNDA. *(to audience)*

THE KING JUST WANTS SOME PRAISE.

KING FREDIPUS.

I HAND-STITCHED EVERY THREAD!

SEGUNDA.

I WISH I COULD ERASE HIS FACE,
BUT I'LL LEAVE THAT UNSAID.

FOR IT WOULD HURT HIS FEELINGS,
HE'D REALLY FEEL THE SLIGHT.
I'LL TELL THE GUY A LITTLE LIE,
AND SAY THAT HE IS RIGHT.

IT'S REALLY JUST POLITE,
TO SAY "THE KING IS RIGHT."

SEGUNDA. *(spoken)* King Fredipus, you look awesome!

KING FREDIPUS. *(spoken)* Oooh. Fredipus the Awesome. I
like it! Hang it there.

(**SEGUNDA** *hangs the new flag.*)

(**KING FREDIPUS** *looks out the window.*)

KING FREDIPUS.

PRIMO! WHAT IS WRONG THAT POOR VILLAGE?
THE CROPS ARE ALL TURNING BROWN.

PRIMO.

IT'S BEEN SO LONG SINCE RAINDROPS FELL.

KING FREDIPUS.

> OKAY, I'LL SAY MY TRICKY SPELL
> AND SEND SOME RAIN TO THIS TOWN.

> (**KING FREDIPUS** *gets his magic wand. He casts a spell.*)

KING FREDIPUS.

> WISHING FAIRIES, COME TOGETHER,
> WE WISH A FIX OF WETTER FEATHER.

> (*Lightning, thunder, and then feathers fall past the window.*)

PRIMO. *(spoken)* Did you say "feather"?

KING FREDIPUS. *(spoken)* I said "weather".

PRIMO.

> OF COURSE YOU DID. I JUST ASSUME
> BECAUSE THE SKY IS RAINING PLUMES,
> AND THE MILLS ARE FULL OF QUILLS,
> AND THE TOWN'S ABOUT TO DROWN IN DANDER.

KING FREDIPUS.

> PRIMO, LET ME SPEAK WITH CANDOR.

> (*He twists* **PRIMO***'s ear.*)

KING FREDIPUS.

> NOW, WHAT DID I SAY?

PRIMO.

> WEATHER! YOU SAID WEATHER!

> (*to audience*) THE KING THINKS HE MADE RAIN.

KING FREDIPUS.

> THAT SPELL WORKED LIKE A CHARM.

PRIMO.

> IF I SAY 'NO,' HE'S SURE TO BLOW
> AND DO ME LOTS OF HARM.

> SO I TELL HIM HE'S CONVINCED ME,
> I'LL SAY I'VE SEEN THE LIGHT.
> TO SAVE MY SKIN I'LL GRIN
> AND SWEAR "THE KING IS ALWAYS RIGHT."

> I'M QUIVERING WITH FRIGHT,
> SO I SAY THE KING IS RIGHT.

*(**PRIMO** pulls the curtain closed.)*

PRIMO, SEGUNDA & TERTIO.
WE HOPE THAT YOU CAN UNDERSTAND.
THAT'S HOW IT IS WITHIN OUR LAND.
AND NO ONE'S EVER THOUGHT TO SAY
IT OUGHT TO BE SOME OTHER WAY.
NO MATTER WHAT HE SAYS,
OR DOES, OR THINKS,
OR MAKES, OR BREAKS,
THE KING MAKES NO MISTAKES!

(END OF SONG 1)

*(Enter **SAMANTHA** with a few feathers stuck in her hair. She is shy and quiet and at first no one notices her.)*

KING FREDIPUS. Say, why hasn't someone brought me my mango juice this morning?

TERTIO. We were just getting to that, Your Perfectness.

SAMANTHA. Hello?

SEGUNDA. There's just so many chores and only the three of us to do them.

SAMANTHA. Excuse me?

PRIMO. But we don't mind. Not at all. I'll just run to the Fantastical Juicing Cart right now.

*(Not watching where he's going, **PRIMO** runs into **SAMANTHA**.)*

PRIMO. Oh! I beg your pardon.

SEGUNDA. Hello, dear. What can we do for you?

SAMANTHA. *(too quietly)* I'm – I'm looking for the king.

PRIMO. What was that?

KING FREDIPUS. Oh dear. She's a mumbler. I can never understand what they're saying.

PRIMO. But you know, she looks strangely familiar.

SEGUNDA. Speak up, dear.

SAMANTHA. *(louder)* I said, I'm looking for the king.

KING FREDIPUS. I am King Fredipus the Awesome. And who are you?

TERTIO. Yes, who are you?

SAMANTHA. Samantha. I'm from the little town just outside your castle.

KING FREDIPUS. I see. And why have you come? Do you need me to solve some mind twisting puzzle? Or outwit some evil prince?

TERTIO. Yes, is it an evil prince?

SAMANTHA. No, not exactly. Something awful has happened.

(She mops her brow wearily.)

SEGUNDA. Oh, the poor dear is exhausted. She must have run all the way to the castle.

SAMANTHA. I am very thirsty.

KING FREDIPUS. Tertio, fetch this young woman something to drink.

TERTIO. Yes, yes. Tertio, get her a drink.

SEGUNDA. Tertio? That's you, hon.

TERTIO. Oh, yeah. I'm Tertio, the king's third advisor. What would you like to drink?

SAMANTHA. What do you have?

*(**TERTIO** crosses to the FJC.)*

TERTIO. We have everything. The Fantastical Juicing Cart can make any sort of drink you'd like. Nothing's too weird or exotic for the old FJC.

SAMANTHA. How about pink lemonade?

TERTIO. *(handing her some)* Lemon with a blush for the little lady.

KING FREDIPUS. Now, tell us what happened.

SAMANTHA. Well, I was on my way to the lake.

PRIMO. That's where I've seen you. You get the water for your town.

SAMANTHA. That's right. And I was walking on the road outside of town when suddenly…

KING FREDIPUS. What? What? Don't keep us in suspense.

SAMANTHA. Well, this may sound hard to believe, but all of a sudden there was a storm of feathers.

(PRIMO *and* SEGUNDA *wince guiltily.*)

KING FREDIPUS. Feathers, you say?

SAMANTHA. Every kind of feather you could imagine. Thousands of them. Crow feathers and duck feathers and I think there were even some ostrich feathers. They kept falling and falling until all the roads were blocked. Now, no one can get in or out of the town.

KING FREDIPUS. How strange. Mysterious, even. I can see why you came to me to solve this problem.

SAMANTHA. My father told me to. He's the bell ringer for our town. He was in the clock tower, and when he saw me on the road he shouted out that I had to tell the king, because I was the only person not trapped by the feathers. I'm sorry to disturb you, King Fredipus, but my town really needs help.

TERTIO. What a coincidence. We were just talking about feathers.

PRIMO & SEGUNDA. Tertio!

TERTIO. Well, we were. See, King Fredipus cast a spell to make it rain, but Primo there thought that the king made a mistake and created a storm of feathers instead.

KING FREDIPUS. *Ahem* but I didn't make a mistake, did I, Tertio?

TERTIO. I was just getting to that, Your Flawlessness. See, Samantha, it wasn't feathers that fell. It was rain.

SAMANTHA. Rain?

KING FREDIPUS. That's right. I gave your town some plain old harmless rain.

SAMANTHA. Oh. But I thought I saw feathers falling.

TERTIO. I know, I know. For a moment there I could have sworn I saw feathers too. But the king said there weren't any, and he's a very smart man. They don't let just anyone be king, do they, sire?

KING FREDIPUS. Nope. You have to be related to another king somehow.

TERTIO. Look Samantha, you and I are just simple people. We don't know half as much as the king knows about anything. So when he says something, we should just believe him.

SAMANTHA. Maybe you're right. Maybe I should just trust the king.

(She notices the feathers in her hair.)

SAMANTHA. Oh but wait, there's some feathers right here.

*(She shows them to **TERTIO**, who in turn shows them to the **KING**.)*

KING FREDIPUS. Take them away! I'm terribly allergic!

*(He sneezes, and as he does so he waves his wand and casts a spell at **PRIMO**. **PRIMO** proceeds to pull a stream of colorful handkerchiefs from his sleeve. He offers them to the king.)*

KING FREDIPUS. Stop playing around! Put those feathers in a glass or something.

*(**TERTIO** puts the feathers in a bottle on the FJC. A moment of silence until **SAMANTHA** speaks timidly.)*

SAMANTHA. Um – excuse me – ?

KING FREDIPUS. What is it? Speak up!

SAMANTHA. Well, I was just wondering – if it didn't rain feathers, then where did those feathers come from?

KING FREDIPUS. For all we know, those feathers fell off your pet rooster.

SAMANTHA. My rooster?

KING FREDIPUS. Does your family own a rooster?

SAMANTHA. Well, yes.

KING FREDIPUS. See? That's the answer. So everything's all right, and you can go home now.

SAMANTHA. Oh. Okay.

(She starts to leave, but stops.)

SAMANTHA. But, my town…

KING FREDIPUS. I'm sure your town is perfectly fine.

TERTIO. Yes. Perfectly fine, perfectly fine. Here, have a look.

(TERTIO *pulls aside the curtain, revealing the town, now buried up to the rooftops in feathers. Only the clock tower peeks out, and perhaps a tiny figure of a man can be seen at its window.*)

SAMANTHA. My poor town! Everything's buried up to the rooftops. Oh, and I can see my father in the clock tower. Father, can you see me?

(*The clock tower rings.*)

SAMANTHA. Oh, you can see me! I made it here to the castle. I'm - I'm trying my best.

(*to* TERTIO)

See, Tertio? My town really is buried in feathers.

TERTIO. Well, that depends on what you mean by "is."

KING FREDIPUS. Look Samantha, I'm very sorry to see that your town is molting or whatever that is, but I didn't mess up my spell. I didn't! I didn't! I didn't!

SEGUNDA. There now, dear King Fredipus. Don't be so cranky. Now, tell me who is the sweetest, happiest, most wonderful monarch in the known world?

KING FREDIPUS. I am.

SEGUNDA. That's right. Excuse me, Samantha, we haven't been properly introduced. I'm Segunda, the king's second advisor.

SAMANTHA. Hi.

SEGUNDA. Yes, hi. The thing is, I'm afraid that you're upsetting the king.

SAMANTHA. Oh, I'm sorry. I didn't mean to.

KING FREDIPUS. Well, you did. You made me feel bad.

SEGUNDA. How would you feel if you thought you'd harmed a whole village of your subjects? Think of the guilt. Think of the remorse.

KING FREDIPUS. Now I feel really bad.

SEGUNDA. And we don't want that, do we? That would be mean. It's so much better to act like a nice and kind young lady who never makes anyone feel bad about anything. Isn't it?

SAMANTHA. I guess so.

SEGUNDA. Well, I know so.

SAMANTHA. The only thing is, my father taught me something different. He says you have to admit your mistakes. Otherwise you never learn from them. And then you just keep making more and more mistakes. Bigger and bigger ones, until finally –

KING FREDIPUS. Stop. I don't want to hear any more!

SEGUNDA. And there's no reason why you should, dear Fredipussycat. Why don't you go write some new laws? That always makes you happy.

KING FREDIPUS. You know, I think I will.

(His advisors bring him pen and parchment.)

KING FREDIPUS. And Law Number One says that there will be no more talking about feathers! It's giving me a headache. Understood?

(He sits down to write more laws.)

SAMANTHA. …Um.

PRIMO. Quiet.

SAMANTHA. But –

PRIMO. Please be quiet, please be quiet, please be quiet!

SAMANTHA. You're Primo, right?

PRIMO. Yes yes yes, I'm Primo, I'm the king's first advisor, and I'm begging you to please stop talking right now!

SAMANTHA. Because you don't want me to hurt the king?

PRIMO. No way, sister. I'm worried about the king hurting you. He's king, and he's a mighty wizard, for goodness sake. Don't you know what he could do to you?

KING FREDIPUS. Oh, Primo. I've just finished making Law Number Two. Can you guess what it is? Can you? All right, I'll tell you. It's the brand new punishment for people who say that the king is wrong.

PRIMO. Ah-ha. Very clever of you, Your Highness. After all, there is no such law on the books at the moment, is there?

KING FREDIPUS. There's never been a need for it.

SAMANTHA. And what is the punishment, if I may ask.

PRIMO. Don't ask. Don't ask.

KING FREDIPUS. Well, there's a choice of three, depending on what the king decides. First, the criminal could be forced to spin around in circles for twenty-four hours. Like so.

*(**KING FREDIPUS** waves his wand, and **PRIMO** begins spinning in circles.)*

KING FREDIPUS. The criminal would probably be dizzy for the rest of the month.

SAMANTHA. How awful.

KING FREDIPUS. Or the king could decide that the criminal will have his face – or her face – magically disfigured for one full year.

SAMANTHA. Disfigured like how?

KING FREDIPUS. Like this.

*(He waves his wand, and **PRIMO** makes the goofiest face he can.)*

SAMANTHA. Oh, that's even worse.

KING FREDIPUS. And finally, my favorite, the king can force the criminal to spend the rest of his natural life thinking that he's a chicken.

*(**KING FREDIPUS** waves his wand, and **PRIMO** starts acting like a chicken: pecking, clucking, scratching.)*

SAMANTHA. Make it stop. I don't want to see any more.

*(**KING FREDIPUS** waves his wand, and **PRIMO** returns to normal.)*

PRIMO. You see now what I'm talking about, Samantha? Look, between you and me, you're right, the king messed up his spell. I saw it happen. But we can't do anything about it. You can't ever say that the king has made a mistake. It's just too dangerous. Understand?

KING FREDIPUS. Well, I've just written Law Number Three, which decrees that because the king is bored, there will be a game of kickball starting right away in the castle courtyard. The sides will be me and Segunda against Primo and Tertio.

PRIMO. Highness, I do still need to run to the lake for water.

KING FREIDPUS. No you don't, Primo, you need to come play with me. Let's go.

SAMANTHA. But shouldn't I be worried about my town?

KING FREDIPUS. Worried? Why that's silly. Isn't it?

TERTIO. Very silly.

SEGUNDA. Zany.

PRIMO. In fact, it's laughable.

> (**KING FREDIPUS, PRIMO, SEGUNDA** *and* **TERTIO** *all laugh.*)

KING FREDIPUS. Everything is fine. After all, I said so. Thank you so much for stopping by. I'm sure you can find your own way out.

> (*All but* **SAMANTHA** *exit.*)

SAMANTHA. Wait! Everything's not fine. Can you see that? Hello?

> (*SONG 2: "SPEAK UP, SAMANTHA"*)

CAN'T ANYBODY SEE?
DOES ANYONE AGREE
THAT OUR KING IS A BIT OF A FOOL?
WELL THERE, I SAID IT,
AND I DON'T REGRET IT.
SOMEONE MUST TAKE HIM TO SCHOOL.
SOMEONE MUST HELP HIM TO RULE,

AND WORK TO CORRECT
HIS MISTAKES WITH RESPECT.
YES, BUT WHO COULD THAT SOMEBODY BE?

(spoken)

Besides me, that is. It can't be me. I don't talk very well, especially to important people. I get so nervous. My tongue turns all…blah! And my palms get…yeesh! And then I start to… *(She hyperventilates, then calms down.)* See? How could I ever make the king listen to a word I said?

(She goes to the window.)

SAMANTHA. I'm sorry, father. I tried.

(sung)

FATHER SAW THAT MAGIC SHOWER,
SAW IT BURY EVERYTHING.
AND HE CALLED DOWN FROM HIS TOWER,
"YOU MUST GO AND TELL THE KING."

(chorus:) HE SAID, "SPEAK UP, SAMANTHA,
WITH WORDS THAT ARE SIMPLE AND TRUE.
DON'T LEAVE THEM UNSPOKEN,
WE'RE DESPERATE FOLK AND
EVERYONE'S COUNTING ON YOU."

BUT NOW I'M HERE AT THE CASTLE,
AND I STAMMER AND I SHAKE.
HE'S THE KING, AND I'M HIS VASSAL,
AND HE NEVER MAKES MISTAKES.

MY FATHER SAID, "SPEAK UP, SAMANTHA.
GO, AND DON'T BE DETERRED.
THE KING MAY NOT HEED YOU,
HIS COURT MAY IMPEDE YOU,
BUT SPEAK UP UNTIL YOU ARE HEARD."

DO I DARE TO BREAK THE SILENCE,
WHEN I'VE GOT SOMETHING TO SAY?
DO I DARE TO SHOW DEFIANCE,
WHEN EVERYONE OBEYS?

DO I DARE TO RAISE MY VOICE,
WHEN I THINK THAT I AM RIGHT?
IT'S ME WHO MAKES THAT CHOICE,
AND I CHOOSE - TO STAY AND FIGHT.

SPEAK UP, SAMANTHA,
AND DON'T MIND THE HOW OR THE WHEN.
AND IF YOU'RE TOO MEEK,
THE FIRST TIME YOU SPEAK,
THEN GO BACK AND SPEAK UP AGAIN.

SPEAK UP, SAMANTHA.
THEY TRUST YOU, SO DON'T LET THEM DOWN.
FINISH YOUR MISSION,
MAKE THE KING LISTEN,
FOR YOUR DAD AND YOUR DEAR LITTLE TOWN.

(END OF SONG 2.)

(KING FREDIPUS, PRIMO, SEGUNDA *and* **TERTIO** *re-enter. The* **KING** *is a little deflated.* **SEGUNDA** *draws the curtain on the window.)*

PRIMO. Wasn't that a fun game, Highness?

KING FREDIPUS. It was all right, I guess.

SEGUNDA. I think you scored more points than ever today.

TERTIO. Well, sure. Because every time he was up we counted it as a home run, no matter what.

KING FREDIPUS. Well, thanks for playing, everyone.

(They spot **SAMANTHA.***)*

KING FREDIPUS. Oh, you're still here. Would you like some more pink lemonade?

SAMANTHA. *(too quietly)* You – you caused the feathers.

KING FREDIPUS. What was that?

SAMANTHA. *(louder)* You caused the storm of feathers, King Fredipus.

(The others gasp.)

KING FREDIPUS. Nonsense.

TERTIO. Yeah, nonsense.

KING FREDIPUS. Thank you, Tertio.

SAMANTHA. What's nonsense is that you think you never make a mistake. Nobody's perfect, Highness. Not even you.

KING FREDIPUS. Samantha, you're making me feel bad. She's mean, Segunda.

SEGUNDA. I know. Cover your ears, dear.

SAMANTHA. Well, I'm sorry if you feel that way, Highness. But you made a mistake, and it's hurting the people in my town. So, I want you to fix what you did wrong. Now, what do you say to that?

KING FREDIPUS. I say, "You're under arrest."

PRIMO. (*to* **SAMANTHA**) See what you did? Now he's going to tell me to seize you.

KING FREDIPUS. Primo, seize her!

(*INSTRUMENTAL:* ***"SEIZE HER."*** **PRIMO** *tries to catch* **SAMANTHA***, but can't.*)

KING FREDIPUS. All of you, seize her!

(*They all try. But their hearts really aren't in it, and* **SAMANTHA** *evades them.*)

KING FREDIPUS. Honestly! Must I do everything myself? Here, try some of the Sandman's yawning dust.

(**KING FREDIPUS** *throws some 'sand' into the air, but* **SAMANTHA** *ducks, and it hits* **PRIMO** *in the face.* **PRIMO** *stops and gives a massive yawn.*)

KING FREDIPUS. Primo! You got in the way!

(*He takes out a small flat object.*)

KING FREDIPUS. Never mind, once she steps on this sticky wicket, Samantha will be too sticky to move.

(**KING FREDIPUS** *tosses the wicket on the ground in front of* **SAMANTHA***, but she jumps over it.* **SEGUNDA** *gets stuck instead.*)

KING FREDIPUS. Segunda! Look what you did.

TERTIO. Don't worry, sire. I shall unstick her!

(He tries to pull her free, but instead **SEGUNDA** *and* **TERTIO** *get stuck together.)*

KING FREDIPUS. All right, now I'm serious. This next spell never fails.

*(***KING FREDIPUS*** *turns around and covers his eyes.)*

One, two, three – red light!

(He turns around and uncovers his eyes. The stage lights dim, and a red special comes up on **SAMANTHA**. **SAMANTHA** *freezes. The chase music ends.)*

Hah! Look everyone, I got her. Hooray for me.

(The **ADVISORS** *clap as best they can.)*

Thank you, thank you. And now, Samantha, for your punishment. Now, which shall it be? I really like that chicken spell. Yes, let's go with that. Ready?

SAMANTHA. King Fredipus, wait!

KING FREDIPUS. Wait? For what?

SAMANTHA. For me to think of something else to say.

KING FREDIPUS. No, I think I'd rather turn you into a chicken. Goodbye, Samantha. It's been very interesting knowing you.

SAMANTHA. Interesting?

KING FREDIPUS. Well, as a matter of fact, yes. I can't remember the last time anyone has spoken to me the way you do.

SAMANTHA. I'll bet it can get pretty boring with everyone agreeing with you all the time, huh?

KING FREDIPUS. Frankly, it's Dullsville. Everyone always saying, "Yes, King," or "You're right, King," or "I couldn't possibly agree more, King." But what you gonna do? The fact is, I'm always right.

(He prepares to wave his wand.)

SAMANTHA. Okay! Okay, okay, okay. Okay, how about this: King Fredipus, I will prove to you that you make mistakes just like everybody else. If I can do that, then you have to let me go free.

KING FREDIPUS. A challenge, eh? How intriguing. What do you think, my advisors? Should I accept?

SEGUNDA. Well, I think it's tacky.

TERTIO. Yeah, tacky.

PRIMO. *(yawns)* I say sleep on it.

KING FREDIPUS. I'm going to do it. Samantha, I accept your challenge. Now, what do we do?

SAMANTHA. I'm still working that out. But I think to begin with, you ought to send your three advisors out of the room.

KING FREDIPUS. Them? Why?

SAMANTHA. I can't tell you until they're gone.

SEGUNDA. Don't listen to her, Highness. It's a trick.

KING FREDIPUS. No no. A trick would be if Samantha suddenly started laying eggs like a Rock Cornish Game Hen, which is what will happen to her if she tries anything funny. You understand me, Samantha?

SAMANTHA. I give you my word I won't.

KING FREDIPUS. All right then. I release you.

*(He waves his wand. **SAMANTHA** can move again.)*

KING FREDIPUS. And you three, stop playing around and go away.

*(He waves his wand. The three **ADVISORS** are released from their previous enchantments, and begin a forced march out the door.)*

SEGUNDA. But Highness –

KING FREDIPUS. But me no buts. Don't come back until you've marched your way once around the whole castle.

TERTIO. This is my least favorite spell.

*(The three **ADVISORS** march off.)*

KING FREDIPUS. Ooh. I'm so excited to win this challenge. Of course you know, you don't have a chance of beating me.

SAMANTHA. Is that a fact, Your Majesty?

KING FREDIPUS. It's a fact, and a law, and a tradition for hundreds of years. And you don't have to ask just me. Everyone else thinks I'm always right too.

SAMANTHA. You mean, like those three advisors?

KING FREDIPUS. Yes, exactly. They agree with me every single time.

SAMANTHA. No, they don't. They just say whatever you want to hear.

KING FREDIPUS. What? Those three have been at my side since I was a little child. I know they'd never lie to me.

SAMANTHA. If that's what you believe, then you're mistaken, Highness.

KING FREDIPUS. Hello, I don't make mistakes.

SAMANTHA. This might be your biggest mistake of all: You don't realize that your advisors – although they are very loyal – are afraid to ever tell you that you're wrong.

KING FREDIPUS. That's simply not true.

SAMANTHA. It is true, Highness. Why, I bet that if you told them that day was night, they'd light candles in the sunshine.

KING FREDIPUS. Ridiculous.

SAMANTHA. If you told them cold was hot, they blow on their ice cubes to cool them down.

KING FREDIPUS. Preposterous.

SAMANTHA. If you told them bitter was sweet, they'd eat the most disgusting thing imaginable and say it was delicious.

KING FREDIPUS. Wrong, wrong, wrong. You are so wrong.

SAMANTHA. No, I'm not.

KING FREDIPUS. Yes, you are.

SAMANTHA. Nuh-uh.

KING FREDIPUS. Yah-huh.

SAMANTHA. Nuh-uh.

KING FREDIPUS. Ooooh! This IS exciting!

SAMANTHA. King Fredipus, I could go over to your Fantastical Juicing Cart right now, and mix up the worst-tasting glass of glop ever mixed up. And – and – *(realizing)* and that's the answer.

KING FREDIPUS. The answer to what?

SAMANTHA. Highness, you like practical jokes, don't you?

KING FREDIPUS. How'd you ever guess?

SAMANTHA. And you'd think it was really funny if we tricked your advisors into drinking something yucky, right?

KING FREDIPUS. You know, that sounds like a lot of fun.

SAMANTHA. Let's do it.

KING FREDIPUS. All right, but don't forget about our challenge.

SAMANTHA. Oh, I won't.

(She goes over to the FJC.)

SAMANTHA. King Fredipus, for you I will make the most foul, the most offensive, the rottenest, stinkiest, disgustingest – The Nastiest Drink in the World!

*(SONG 3: "**THE NASTIEST DRINK IN THE WORLD**")*

*(As **SAMANTHA** and **KING FREDIPUS** sing, they add various ingredients into the big bowl.)*

SAMANTHA.

JUST TAKE TWO PINTS OF APPLE JUICE,
AND ADD IN GREASE OF WILD GOOSE.
MIX CHOCOLATE FUDGE AND TUNA FISH,
WITH VINEGAR AND LICORICE.

CHEWING GUM AND CHILI BEAN,
SUGARPLUM AND MARGARINE.
SOUR, SALTY, BITTER, SWEET.
WITH EVERY FLAVOR YOU CAN EAT.

THEN YOU POUR IT OVER ICE,
GARNISH WITH A PICKLE SLICE.
THERE, THE NASTY DRINK IS DONE.

KING FREDIPUS. *(spoken)* Done? Already?

SAMANTHA. It's pretty nasty, Your Highness. My eyes are starting to water just from being near it.

KING FREDIPUS. We can't stop now. I'm having so much fun. Besides, all your ingredients were actually food. The Fantastical Juicing Cart can make juice out of anything. Now, it's my turn, and I'm going to add some really nasty stuff. Look out!

(sung)

THE SLIME THAT'S LEFT BY PASSING SNAILS,
THE GRIME BENEATH YOUR FINGERNAILS.
SOME YELLOW SNOW AND EARTHWORM SOUP,
AND CREAM OF YEAR-OLD PIGEON POOP.
EAR WAX, DOG SNACKS, SHINY MEAT,
JELLY SCRAPED FROM SMELLY FEET.
INKBLOTS, BLOODCLOTS, CIGARETTES
EYEBALLS, HAIRBALLS, ARMPIT SWEAT.

THEN YOU STIR IT WITH A FORK,
AND YOU STOP IT WITH A CORK.
'CAUSE THAT'S HOW THE NASTY DRINK IS DONE.

KING FREDIPUS. *(spoken)* Except it doesn't feel like it's done, does it?

SAMANTHA. I suppose it's possible to make this drink even nastier. But I'm fresh out of ideas.

KING FREDIPUS. Me too. I know! Let's ask them!

(He points to the audience.)

SAMANTHA. That's a great idea!

(to the audience) Can you think of some disgusting things to put in our nasty drink?

*(**SAMANTHA** and **KING FREDIPUS** solicit some suggestions from the audience. And whatever the audience suggests, **SAMANTHA** and **KING FREDIPUS** pull from the Fantastical Juicing Cart in liquefied or powdered form.)*

KING FREDIPUS. *(sung)*
HAVE WE GOT THE EELS AND MUSTARD?
AND THE SPINACH AND THE CUSTARD?

SAMANTHA.

AND THE SWEAT IS IN HERE TOO.
AND THE SLIME AND GRIME AND GLUE.

BOTH.

IT'S ALL HERE!

SAMANTHA.

THEN YOU SPRINKLE IN SOME SALT,
AND YOU WHIP IT LIKE A MALT.

KING FREDIPUS.

THEN YOU ADD A CUP OF FLOUR,
AND YOU STIR IT FOR AN HOUR.

SAMANTHA.

THEN YOU COVER IT WITH FOIL,
AND YOU BRING IT TO A BOIL.

KING FREDIPUS.

THEN YOU ADD A COUPLE SNEEZES,
AND YOU PICK OUT ALL THE PIECES.

SAMANTHA.

THEN YOU COOK IT 'TIL IT'S BLACKER,
AND YOU SPREAD IT ON A CRACKER.

KING FREDIPUS.

THEN YOU STRAIN OUT ALL THE PULP,
AND YOU DOWN IT IN ONE GULP.

BOTH.

AND THAT'S HOW THE NASTY DRINK IS –
THAT'S HOW THE NASTY DRINK IS DONE!

(END OF SONG 3)

KING FREDIPUS. I hear my advisors coming now. This is going to be hilarious!

SAMANTHA. One last thing, King Fredipus. In order to get them to drink it, you have to tell Primo, Segunda and Tertio that you think this drink tastes great.

KING FREDIPUS. I tell them it tastes great.

SAMANTHA. Exactly.

KING FREDIPUS. Got it.

(**PRIMO, SEGUNDA** *and* **TERTIO** *march back onstage.*)

PRIMO. Highness, while we were away, I noticed that the moat has completely evaporated. We're almost totally out of water.

KING FREDIPUS. Yes, yes, wonderful. Welcome back, my three loyal advisors.

*(He waves his wand. The **ADVISORS** are set free from their marching spell.)*

KING FREDIPUS. Samantha has shown me how to make the most - ah - delicious drink ever.

*(**KING FREDIPUS** giggles. **SAMANTHA** joins in.)*

SEGUNDA. You and Samantha seem to have made up. How nice.

PRIMO. Maybe no punishment will be necessary?

KING FREDIPUS. We'll see. We'll see. But for now, you must all have a cup. Trust me, you've never tasted anything like it before.

*(**KING FREDIPUS** chortles. He hands **PRIMO** a glass.)*

KING FREDIPUS. Go on, Primo. Drink up.

*(**PRIMO** looks at the drink dubiously.)*

PRIMO. Your Highness has – experienced – this beverage for himself?

KING FREDIPUS. Yes, yes. And I'm telling you, Primo, it's great.

PRIMO. Oh, excuse me. Ladies first.

*(**PRIMO** hands the glass to **SEGUNDA**. **KING FREDIPUS** hands **PRIMO** a second glass. **SEGUNDA** sniffs the drink and makes a face.)*

SEGUNDA. Well, the aroma certainly is – robust.

KING FREDIPUS. Bottoms up, Segunda.

SEGUNDA. Oh, but poor Tertio looks so thirsty after our march. You first, dear.

*(**SEGUNDA** hands **TERTIO** the glass. **PRIMO** hands **SEGUNDA** his glass. **KING FREDIPUS** gives **PRIMO** a third glass. **TERTIO** studies the glass for a second.)*

TERTIO. Well, if it's good enough for King Fredipus, it's good enough for me.

*(SONG 4: "**IT'S GREAT!**")*

(TERTIO *drinks. He gags.)*

TERTIO.

IT'S GREAT!

KING FREDIPUS.

IT'S GREAT?

TERTIO.

IT'S GREAT, JUST LIKE YOU SAY,
AND IF I GAG AND CHOKE A BIT,
I LOVE IT ANYWAY.

KING FREDIPUS. *(spoken)* Bottom's up, Segunda.

(SEGUNDA *drinks. She sticks her tongue out in horror.)*

SEGUNDA.

IT'S GREAT!

KING FREDIPUS.

IT'S GREAT?

SEGUNDA.

IT REALLY IS DIVINE.
IT DANCES ON MY TASTEBUDS LIKE
SOME GRAY AND LUMPY WINE.

KING FREDIPUS. *(spoken)* Well, go on, Primo.

(PRIMO *drinks, and immediately spits it back into the cup. Realizing what he's done, he then drinks it again.)*

PRIMO.

IT'S GREAT!

KING FREDIPUS.

IT'S GREAT?

PRIMO.

WHAT TASTE, WHAT TANG, WHAT SPICE!
I ONLY SPAT IT OUT AGAIN
SO I COULD DRINK IT TWICE.

(PRIMO, SEGUNDA *and* **TERTIO** *go into a round.)*

PRIMO, SEGUNDA AND TERTIO.

IT'S GREAT!

KING FREDIPUS.

IT'S GREAT?

PRIMO, SEGUNDA & TERIO.

IT'S GREAT JUST LIKE YOU SAY,

TERTIO. *(simultaneously)*

AND IF I GAG AND CHOKE A BIT,

AND IF I GAG AND CHOKE A BIT,

AND IF I GAG AND CHOKE A BIT,

I LOVE IT ANYWAY.

SEGUNDA. *(simultaneously)*

IT DANCES ON MY TASTEBUDS LIKE

IT DANCES ON MY TASTEBUDS LIKE

SOME GRAY AND LUMPY WINE.

PRIMO. *(simultaneously)*

I ONLY SPAT IT OUT AGAIN

SO I COULD DRINK IT TWICE.

KING FREDIPUS.

IT'S GREAT!

PRIMO, SEGUNDA AND TERTIO.

IT'S GREAT!

KING FREDIPUS.

YOU REALLY THINK IT'S GREAT?

PRIMO, SEGUNDA AND TERTIO.

IT'S GREAT! IT'S GREAT! WE REALLY THINK IT'S GREAT!

KING FREDIPUS.

I KNOW YOU WOULDN'T CHEER "IT'S GREAT!"

BECAUSE I WANT TO HEAR IT'S GREAT.

IT'S ABSOLUTELY CLEAR, IT'S GREAT.

PRIMO, SEGUNDA AND TERTIO.

IT'S GREAT!

KING FREDIPUS.

IT REALLY MUST BE TRUE.

AND IF YOU LIKE IT ALL THAT MUCH,

THEN I MUST HAVE SOME TOO!

(END OF SONG 4)

(**KING FREDIPUS** *prepares to drink a huge glass of the stuff.*)

SAMANTHA. King Fredipus, stop!

(*He stops.*)

SAMANTHA. What are you doing?

KING FREDIPUS. I'm just – I was going to – Those three said it was great.

SAMANTHA. But you know it isn't.

(*to the audience*) We know the drink tastes bad, right?

(*to King Fredipus*) Your advisors aren't telling you the truth, King Fredipus.

PRIMO. Of course we are!

SEGUNDA. The drink is delicious.

TERTIO. Can I have some more?

(**PRIMO** *and* **SEGUNDA** *look at* **TERTIO.**)

SEGUNDA. (*under her breath*) Weirdo.

SAMANTHA. Highness, you said your advisors never lied to you. But I just proved that they do. You were mistaken. And that means I've won the challenge.

KING FREDIPUS. No you haven't. You haven't won a thing. I'll show you.

(*He is about to drink.*)

SAMANTHA. Highness. Remember what I said before. You have to admit your mistakes, or else you'll just keep making more of them.

(**KING FREDIPUS** *looks from his advisors to* **SAMANTHA.** *Then he drains a huge glass of the stuff, far more than anyone else has.*)

KING FREDIPUS. You know, it's really not that...

(*INSTRUMENTAL: "THE KING DRINKS"*)

(Suddenly, the nastiness of the drink hits **KING FREDIPUS** *like a shot. He goes rigid. His crown flies off his head. Driven bonkers by the drink, he bounces about the stage like a cartoon: babbling, convulsing, howling, barking, turning cartwheels or banging his head against the wall. He then begins pitching to and fro, in danger of falling.* **PRIMO, SEGUNDA** *and* **TERTIO** *race about the stage, frantically trying to get beneath him. They catch him just as he collapses.)*

KING FREDIPUS. Oh, that's so nasty.

(He then passes out.)

PRIMO. Ahhh…King Fredipus? Hello?

(The three advisors peer closely at him. **KING FREDIPUS** *wakes with a start.)*

KING FREDIPUS. Oh, what an awful taste! I've got to get it out of my mouth! Mouthwash! Where's the mouthwash?

(He goes over to the FJC. He finds some mouthwash and gargles.)

Yuck. My mouth still tastes nasty! Where's my toothbrush?

(He produces a toothbrush and brushes his teeth. When he's finished, he brushes his tongue.)

TERTIO. Remember, little circles, Your Highness.

KING FREDIPUS. Why did you all let me drink that?

TERTIO. Why? Because it's the most delicious drink in the world.

KING FREDIPUS. No, it's not! It's terrible. It's worse than terrible. It's the most nauseating thing that anyone has put in his mouth ever!

TERTIO. It is? Well, that would explain why I kept choking on it.

KING FREDIPUS. Dunce! I only drank it because you three all said it was great.

SEGUNDA. But we only said it was great because you said it was great.

PRIMO. I'm so confused!

KING FREDIPUS. Well, I'll explain it to you. It seems that all this time you three have been lying to me. "It's great" indeed. Get out, you're all fired.

SEGUNDA. Highness, please.

KING FREDIPUS. Out, I said!

SAMANTHA. But I didn't mean for this to happen.

PRIMO. What will I tell Mom?

*(The **ADVISORS** sadly exit.)*

KING FREDIPUS. That goes for you too, Samantha.

SAMANTHA. Don't you think you're being a little hard on them?

KING FREDIPUS. I can't believe I still have this awful taste in my mouth. There must be something here that can take it away.

(He starts going through the FJC, sampling what he finds.)

KING FREDIPUS. What are you still doing here? I told you to leave.

SAMANTHA. I can't. Not until you fix what you did wrong.

KING FREDIPUS. "Wrong." That's all you can say, isn't it? "King Fredipus is wrong. King Fredipus made a mistake." I know what you really mean. You think that I'm incompetent.

SAMANTHA. No, I don't.

KING FREDIPUS. You think I don't have the right stuff.

SAMANTHA. I never believed that.

KING FREDIPUS. Oh, maybe you'd say I could get by as the Duke of Earl or the Aristocrat formerly known as Prince. But when it comes right down to it, you don't think I'm good enough to be King of Baloneya.

(He finds an empty glass.)

KING FREDIPUS. Hey, this glass is empty. And so are these. Where has all the water gone?

SAMANTHA. It hasn't rained in three months, Highness.

KING FREDIPUS. I need something, anything.

> *(SONG 5: **"SNEEZE ATTACK"**)*

> *(**KING FREDIPUS** begins guzzling whatever he can find, not even looking at the glasses.)*

SAMANTHA.

> KING FREDIPUS, PLEASE SLOW DOWN!
> AND CAREFUL WHAT YOU DO.
> NOT THAT GLASS, NO NOT THAT GLASS!

> *(He has tried to drink from the glass with the feathers, and the feathers have gone in his mouth, and right up his nose.)*

KING FREDIPUS. OH NO – OH NO! – ACHOOOOOO!

> *(As he sneezes, he waves his wand. The sign reading "The King is Always Right" tips over.)*

SAMANTHA.

> LOOK, YOUR SIGN HAS BEEN UPENDED.

KING FREDIPUS.

> HEY, THAT'S NOT WHAT I INTENDED!

> *(He sneezes, waves his wand again. The flag is yanked offstage.)*

SAMANTHA.

> NOW YOUR FLAG JUST UP AND WENT.

KING FREDIPUS.

> IT MUST HAVE BEEN AN ACCIDENT!

> *(He sneezes, waves his wand again. SFX: spell music. From a concealed slit in the wall, a hand emerges. It grabs **SAMANTHA**.)*

SAMANTHA.

> LOOK OUT, IT'S A MAGIC HAND!

KING FREDIPUS.

> THIS REALLY ISN'T WHAT I PLANNED!

*(He continues to sneeze, and a second, third and fourth hand emerge to fight **SAMANTHA**.)*

(He sneezes waving the wand at himself. SFX: Spell music. He starts spinning and dancing.)

KING FREDIPUS.

OH NO! MY MAGIC WAND,
IS FORCING ME TO DANCE.

*(**KING FREDIPUS**' flailing about accidentally brings his hands to his posterior, and he realizes:)*

KING FREDIPUS.

AND WHAT'S WORSE, I THINK I'VE FOUND
A HOLE IN MY SILKEN PANTS!

*(Dance break: **KING FREDIPUS** dances comically while **SAMANTHA** duels with the magic hands.)*

*(**SAMANTHA** struggles to reach the wand.)*

KING FREDIPUS.

HELP ME, SAMANTHA.

SAMANTHA.

I'M TRYING.

KING FREDIPUS.

REACH ME, SAMANTHA!

SAMANTHA.

I'M REACHING!
ALMOST THERE. CAN NEARLY TOUCH.
(spoken)

Got it!

*(She grabs the wand. The **KING** stops dancing. The hands release **SAMANTHA** and disappear.)*

KING FREDIPUS.

THANK YOU VERY MUCH!
(END OF SONG 5)

KING FREDIPUS. Are you all right?

SAMANTHA. I think so. What a mess.

KING FREDIPUS. It really is. How could such a thing have happened? Wait, wait. I know the answer to that. I did it. All of it. By mistake. I made a mistake.

SAMANTHA. Maybe even more than one.

(*PRIMO, SEGUNDA and TERTIO enter.*)

SEGUNDA. Your Highness? We found some mint leaves in the royal garden. That should take the taste of the nasty drink away.

(*She gives him some. He eats it.*)

KING FREDIPUS. Thank you. Oh. That's so much better.

PRIMO. We also wanted you to know we're sorry if we let you down.

TERTIO. And now, goodbye. Goodbye forever!

KING FREDIPUS. Wait, Tertio. You three shouldn't be leaving. I should!

TERTIO. You? But why?

KING FREDIPUS. Because of all the awful mistakes I've made.

TERTIO. Don't be silly. Everyone knows King Fredipus doesn't make mistakes.

KING FREDIPUS. Yes, I do.

PRIMO. But the law says —

KING FREDIPUS. Forget the law. I'm telling you I make mistakes. Lots and lots of them.

TERTIO. I think he means it.

SEGUNDA. He does. He really does mean it.

PRIMO. Oh, how we've prayed for this day!

KING FREDIPUS. Don't you understand? I'm king. I'm not supposed to make mistakes. (*sobbing*) I'm a bad king!

TERTIO. But, Majesty, we don't think you're bad.

KING FREDIPUS. You don't?

SEGUNDA. We think that for the first time, you're learning something really important. Thanks to Samantha.

PRIMO. Making mistakes is how you learn, Sire.

KING FREDIPUS. So you mean, it's okay that I'm not always right?

SEGUNDA. Nobody is.

KING FREDIPUS. Hey, that's right. Everyone makes mistakes. I'm just like everyone else. I don't have to be perfect. Oh, what a relief!

PRIMO. And you know, you're the first King of Baloneya ever to admit that. Maybe now you can fix some of the things that you and your ancestors have done wrong.

SAMANTHA. And that's what's important, Highness: to fix your mistakes when you realize them.

KING FREDIPUS. You know, you're right, Samantha. And I'm going to start by fixing what I did to your town.

(He peeks out the curtain.)

KING FREDIPUS. Just look at all those feathers. I know, I'll create a storm. A really big storm. And it'll wash them all away.

SAMANTHA. Maybe it could even fill all the wells up?

KING FREDIPUS. It should. Now, let me try to do that spell again. *(nervously)* That very tricky spell. The one I messed up before.

SAMANTHA. King Fredipus? Are you okay?

KING FREDIPUS. What if I make a mistake again?

SAMANTHA. You can't let that hold you back.

KING FREDIPUS. No, you don't understand. Your town might be buried in feathers forever.

SAMANTHA. Oh. We don't want that.

KING FREDIPUS. I'm thinking. I'm thinking. I've got it! If a lot of people say the spell with me, it won't matter if some of us mess it up. But where will we find so many people?

*(The **CAST** ad libs suggestions but the people suggested are all unavailable. For example: "I know this guy in Human Resources." "It's his day off." Until…)*

SAMANTHA. *(indicating the audience)* Hey! Let's ask them!

KING FREDIPUS. Yes! That will work.

(to the audience) Would you help us please? I'm going to say the spell, and then you all repeat it back to me. Ready?

KING FREDIPUS.

WISHING FAIRIES, COME TOGETHER,
WE WISH A FIX OF WETTER WEATHER.

(LFX: Lightning. SFX: Thunder, and the sound of rain falling.)

KING FREDIPUS. Listen! I think we've done it.

(They pull aside the curtain to reveal the town, now back to normal.)

SAMANTHA. My town. My beautiful town. Everything's okay again! Thank you so much, King Fredipus!

KING FREDIPUS. No, thank you, Samantha. All of us here are in your debt.

*(**KING FREDIPUS** leads the advisors in bowing to **SAMANTHA**.)*

SAMANTHA. You're very welcome.

(She catches sight of her father in the window.)

Look, there's my father. Father, I did it! I got the King to listen!

(The clock bell rings.)

KING FREDIPUS. Samantha, I was wondering if you'd consider staying on here at the palace.

SAMANTHA. Staying? What for?

KING FREDIPUS. Why, to be one of my royal advisors, of course. Today you've given me some of the best advice ever.

*(SONG 6: **"FINALE"**)*

KING FREDIPUS.

WELCOME TO BALONEYA

OUR FUTURE'S FAIR AND BRIGHT.

A PAGE HAS TURNED BECAUSE I'VE LEARNED

THAT NO ONE'S ALWAYS RIGHT.

SAMANTHA.

MY FATHER SAID "SPEAK UP, SAMANTHA,"

AND HE WAS SO RIGHT ALL ALONG.

SO AFTER TODAY

WHEN I'VE SOMETHING TO SAY

YOU CAN BET I'LL SPEAK LOUDLY AND STRONG.

PRIMO, SEGUNDA & TERTIO.

THAT'S GREAT!

THAT'S GREAT!

WE REALLY THINK THAT'S GREAT!

AND NOW WE'LL NEVER CHEER IT'S GREAT,

WHEN SOMEONE WANTS TO HEAR IT'S GREAT,

BUT ONLY WHEN IT'S CLEAR IT'S GREAT.

ALL.

NOW ALL IS WELL.

(The clock tower bell "rings".)

ALL.

THE CLOCK BELL IN BALONEYA

RINGS "FAREWELL FROM BALONEYA."

THE TALE OF THE NASTY DRINK IS DONE!

(END OF SONG 6)

(End of play.)

PROPERTIES

Fantastical Juicing Cart (FJC) with a mixing bowl and assorted cups
Bucket and ladle
A sign reading "The King is always Right"
King's wand
National flag of Baloneya
New "King Fredipus" flag
Feathers
Sandman's yawning dust
Sticky wicket (a flat square)
Toothbrush
Mintleaves

OTHER TITLES AVAILABLE FROM BAKER'S PLAYS

THE GREAT GREY GHOST OF OLD SPOOK LANE

Anne Phillips

TYA, Children's Musical / 4 boys, 4 girls, 1 lead boy or girl, 1 older student or adult male / Simple Set

The Great Grey Ghost of Old Spook Lane is about a little boy, Roger, who is new in town. The kids at school tell him about a haunted house and dare him to go in. Roger feels he has to do it to get "in" with the gang. So on a rainy night they all meet and push him in through a window. The lights go on. The house isn't empty. An elderly man lives there quietly. He used to be a sound effects man back in radio days he has all the equipment in the basement. They play a trick on the kids and invite them back for dinner. The house is filled with scary sound effects as the "Ghost" serves his "Ghostly Repast" of evil eye soup, phantom pie, etc. Everyone is scared except brave Roger.

The kids learn a lesson about accepting new people and Roger learns there are limits to what you should do to be accepted.

www.ingramcontent.com/pod-product-compliance
Lightning Source LLC
Chambersburg PA
CBHW070420120726
47909CB00005B/1736